A Painter

by Douglas Florian

Greenwillow Books New York

Many thanks to Mikel Glass and my wife, Marie,
for their help on this book

Watercolor paints and colored pencils were used for the full-color art. The text type is Bryn Mawr Book.

Copyright © 1993 by Douglas Florian

All rights reserved. No part of this book may be reproduced or utilized in any form or by any means, electronic or mechanical, including photocopying, recording, or by any information storage and retrieval system, without permission in writing from the Publisher, Greenwillow Books, a division of William Morrow & Company, Inc., 1350 Avenue of the Americas, New York, NY 10019.

Printed in Hong Kong by South China Printing Company (1988) Ltd.

First Edition
10 9 8 7 6 5 4 3 2 1

Library of Congress Cataloging-in-Publication Data
Florian, Douglas.
A painter / by Douglas Florian.
p. cm.
Summary: Briefly describes the tools of a painter, his subject matter, and the feelings he feels as he creates pictures.
ISBN 0-688-11872-0 (trade)
ISBN 0-688-11873-9 (lib. bdg.)
1. Art—Juvenile literature.
[1. Art. 2. Artists. 3. Occupations.]
I. Title.
N7440.F66 1993
750—dc20
92-29583 CIP AC

For my father, Harold Florian,
a painter

A painter creates pictures.

With sticks of charcoal
he can draw long, swirling lines.

With watercolors
he can paint a mosaic of colors.

With oils he can paint
rich patterns and textures.

With pastels he can draw
strokes of shimmering light.

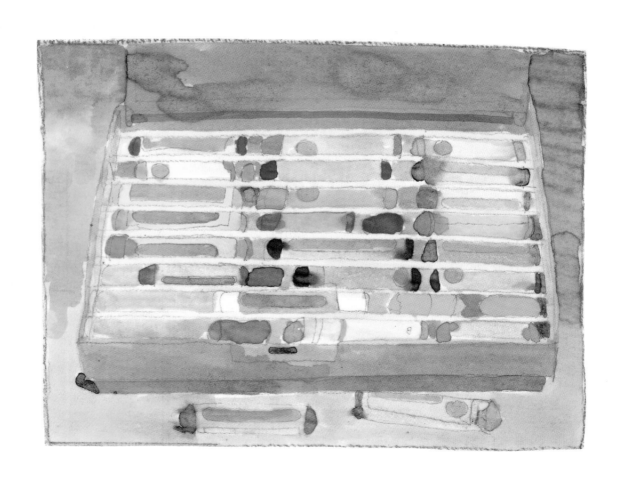

With paper, scissors, and glue
he can create a collage of shapes.

He can work large

or small.

A painter can paint what he sees:

a busy street,

a grove of trees,

children playing.

A painter can paint what he feels:

sadness,

anger,

joy.

He can paint from memory.

He can paint from his imagination.

In different ways,

day after day,

a painter creates pictures.

A PAINTER'S MATERIALS

Linseed oil improves the flow and transparency of oil paint.

An easel holds the canvas. It can be raised and lowered to hold different sizes of paintings.

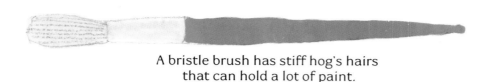

A bristle brush has stiff hog's hairs that can hold a lot of paint.

A sable brush has fine, soft hairs. It is good for smooth strokes and details.

A palette knife mixes color and scrapes away paint.

A palette is used to mix paint. The thumb hole helps you hold it.

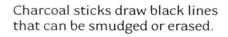

Charcoal sticks draw black lines that can be smudged or erased.

Pastel sticks come in many different colors. They can be blended together.

Drawing pens come in different sizes and shapes. They are dipped into ink.

Turpentine is used to thin oil colors and clean brushes.

Oil paints dry slowly and have a glowing richness.

Acrylic paints mix with water. They dry very quickly.

Watercolor paints also mix with water. They are usually painted on paper.